williambee

williambee
Stanley's
Store

Published by
PEACHTREE PUBLISHING COMPANY INC.
1700 Chattahoochee Avenue
Atlanta, Georgia 30318-2112
PeachtreeBooks.com

First published in Great Britain in 2017 by Jonathan Cape, an imprint of Penguin Random House Children's
First United States version published in 2017 by Peachtree Publishing Company Inc.

First trade paperback edition published in 2018

The illustrations were rendered digitally.

Printed and bound in October 2022 at Leo Paper, Heshan, China.
10 9 8 7 6 5 4 3 2 1 (hardcover)
10 9 8 7 6 5 4 3 2 (trade paperback)
HC ISBN: 978-1-68263-613-8
PB ISBN: 978-1-68263-058-7

Library of Congress Cataloging-in-Publication Data

Names: Bee, William, author, illustrator.
Title: Stanley's store / William Bee.
Description: First edition. | Atlanta, Georgia : Peachtree Publishers, [2017] |
Summary: During a busy day at the grocery store, Stanley uses a fork lift to remove fruits and
vegetables from a truck, makes a display, and helps customers.
Identifiers: LCCN 2016020433 | ISBN 9781561458684
Subjects: | CYAC: Grocery trade—Fiction. | Stores, Retail—Fiction. | Hamsters—Fiction. | Rodents—Fiction.
Classification: LCC PZ7.B38197 Sx 2017 | DDC [E]—dc23 LC record available at
https://lccn.loc.gov/2016020433

williambee
Stanley's
Store

Ω PEACHTREE
ATLANTA

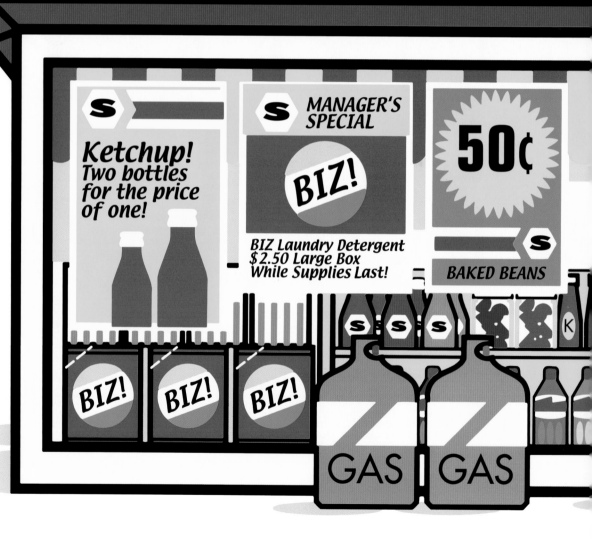

Ketchup! Two bottles for the price of one!

MANAGER'S SPECIAL

BIZ!

BIZ Laundry Detergent $2.50 Large Box While Supplies Last!

50¢

BAKED BEANS

BIZ! BIZ! BIZ!

GAS GAS

It's going to be another busy day at Stanley's Store.

Stanley is unloading fresh fruits and vegetables from the truck.

His yellow forklift goes
PEEPPEEPPEEPPEEPEEP.

Hattie helps Myrtle pick out cheese.

Myrtle likes round cheese and
square cheese and triangular cheese.
In fact, she likes any shape of cheese!

Shamus and Little Woo are on their weekly shopping trip. Little Woo rides in the cart.

He is just the right height to reach the sweets. Little Woo loves shopping.

Myrtle wants some nice bread
to go with her cheese.

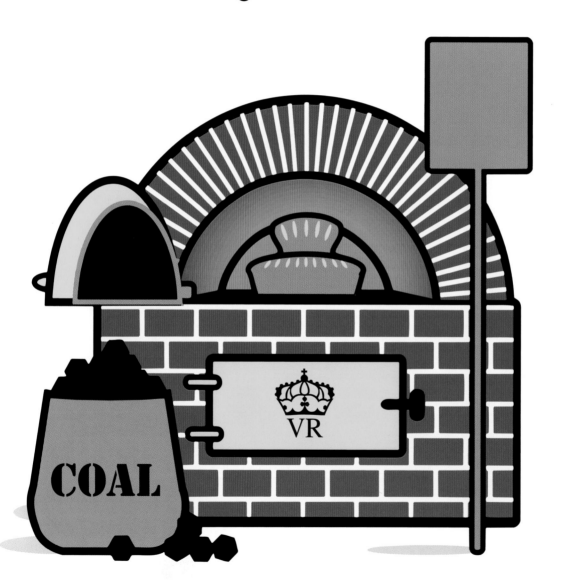

Gabriel gives her a cottage loaf
fresh from the oven.
Mind your fingers, Myrtle. It's still hot!

Stanley built a beautiful display
of fruits and vegetables.
Well done, Stanley!

Oh dear! Charlie isn't looking
where he's going...

...silly Charlie!

Red apples, green watermelons, purple plums, and lovely yellow bananas are everywhere!

At the cash register, Stanley rings up Shamus and Little Woo's groceries.

What a lot of cookies
and chocolates...

Myrtle bought too much
cheese to carry.

How will she get it all home?

Luckily for Myrtle,
Stanley's Store delivers.

Thank you, Stanley! Thank you, Hattie!

Well! What a busy day!

Time for supper!
Time for a bath!

And time for bed!
Goodnight, Stanley.

Stanley

If you liked **Stanley's Store** then you'll
love these other books about Stanley:

Stanley the Builder
HC: $14.99 / 978-1-56145-801-1

Stanley the Mailman
HC: $14.95 / 978-1-56145-867-7

Stanley's Fire Engine
HC: $14.99 / 978-1-68263-214-7

Stanley's Garage
HC: $14.95 / 978-1-56145-804-2

Stanley's School
HC: $16.99 / 978-1-68263-602-2

Stanley's Library
HC: $14.99 / 978-1-68263-313-7

Stanley the Farmer
HC: $14.95 / 978-1-56145-803-5

Stanley's Train
HC: $16.99 / 978-1-68263-603-9

Stanley's Boat
HC: $16.99 / 978-1-68263-571-1

Stanley's Diner
HC: $14.99 / 978-1-56145-802-8

Stanley's Park
HC: $16.99 / 978-1-68263-572-8